fairies

The Trouble with Tink

This edition published by Parragon in 2011

Parragon
Queen Street House
4 Queen Street
Bath, BA1 1HE, UK

ISBN 978-1-4454-2261-9

Printed in China.

Disney
fairies

The Trouble with Tink

WRITTEN BY

Kiki Thorpe

ILLUSTRATED BY

Judith Holmes Clarke
&
The Disney Storybook Artists

Bath · New York · Singapore · Hong Kong · Cologne · Delhi
Melbourne · Amsterdam · Johannesburg · Auckland · Shenzhen

Tinker Bell sat in her workshop, frowning at a copper pot. The pot had been squashed nearly flat on one side. Tink was trying to determine how to make it right again. Tink was a pots-and-pans fairy, and her greatest joy came from fixing things.

Ping! Ping! Ping! Beneath Tink's hammer the copper moved back into its original shape.

Tink had almost finished when she saw a dark figure silhouetted in her doorway. The edges of the silhouette sparkled.

"Oh, hi Terence," said Tink.

Terence was a dust-talent sparrow man. He handed out the fairy dust that allowed Never Land's fairies to fly. As a result, he was dustier than most fairies and he sparkled all the time.

"Hi, Tink. I see you're working. Are you almost done? That's a nice pot," Terence said.

"It's Violet's pot. They're dyeing spider silk tomorrow and she needs it for boiling the dye," Tink replied.

"That's right, tomorrow is dyeing

day," said Terence. "I saw the harvest-talents bringing in the blueberries for the dye earlier. They've got a good crop this year..."

As Terence rambled on, Tink looked longingly at the copper pot. She picked up her hammer, then put it back down. It would be rude to start tapping right now, she thought.

"Anyway, Tink, I just wanted to let you know that they're starting a game of tag in the meadow. I thought maybe you'd like to join in," Terence finished.

Tink's wingtips quivered. It had been ages since there had been a game of fairy tag.

She glanced down at the pot again. The dent was nearly smooth. Tink thought she could easily play a game of tag and still have time to finish her work before dinner.

Tink slipped her tinker's hammer into a loop on her belt and smiled at Terence. "Let's go," she said.

When Tink and Terence got to the meadow, the game was already in full swing. Everywhere spots of bright colour wove in and out of the tall grass as fairies darted after each other.

In fairy tag, the fairies and sparrow men all use their talents to try and win. And when a fairy is tagged, by being tapped on the head and told "choose you", that fairy's whole talent group becomes "chosen".

As Tink and Terence joined the game, a huge drop of water came hurtling through the air at them. The water-talent fairies had been "chosen", Tink realized.

The water fairies hurled balls of water that burst like water balloons and dampened the other fairies' wings. This slowed them down, which helped the water fairies gain on them.

But the other talents had quickly organized their defences. The animal-talent fairies had rounded up a crew of chipmunks to ride when their

wings got too wet to fly. The light-talent fairies bent the sunshine, so rays of light blinded the fairies chasing them. Tink saw that the pots-and-pans fairies had used washtubs to create makeshift catapults to catch the balls of water and fling them back at the water fairies.

Suddenly, Tink heard a voice above her call, "Watch out, Tinker Bell! I'll choose you!" She looked up. Her friend Rani, a water-talent fairy, was circling above her on the back of a dove.

Rani lifted her arm and hurled a water ball. It splashed harmlessly on the ground. "I'm such a terrible shot!" Rani cried happily.

"Choose you!"

The shout rang through the meadow. All the fairies stopped in midflight and turned. A water-talent fairy named Tally had "chosen" Jerome, a dust-talent sparrow man.

"Dust-talent!" Jerome sang out.

Tink caught sight of Terence a few feet away. Terence grinned at her. She smiled back – and then she bolted.

Tink dove into an azalea bush. Terence was right on her heels. She dashed towards an opening in the leaves and headed back to the open meadow.

But suddenly, the twigs in front of her closed like a gate. With a flick of fairy dust, Terence had closed the branches of the bush. Tink was trapped.

"Choose you," Terence said, placing his hand on Tink's head.

Just then, a shout rang out across the meadow: "Hawk!"

At once, Tink and Terence dropped down under the azalea bush's branches. Tink could see the other fairies also ducking for cover. The entire meadow seemed to hold its breath as the hawk's shadow moved across it.

When the hawk was gone, the fairies slowly came out of their hiding places. But the mood had changed. The game of tag was over.

"I must finish Violet's pot before dinner," Tink told Terence. "Thank you for telling me about the game."

"I'm really glad you came, Tink," said Terence. He gave her a sparkling smile, but Tink didn't see it. She was already flying away.

As she neared her workshop, she reached for the tinker's hammer hanging on her belt. Her fingertips touched the leather loop.

Tink stopped flying. Frantically, she ran her fingers over the belt loop again and again. Her hammer was gone!

2

Tink flew back to the meadow.
Her eyes darted this way and that,
hoping to catch a glimmer of metal in
the tall grass.

"Fool," Tink told herself. "You
foolish, foolish fairy."

Just then, her eyes fell on the
azalea bush. Of course! Tink thought.
I must have dropped it when I was
dodging Terence.

Tink flew to the bush. She checked the ground beneath it and then she checked each branch. But the hammer was nowhere in sight.

Fighting back tears, Tink searched the meadow inch by inch. She parted the petals of wildflowers. She peered into rabbit burrows. She looked everywhere she could think of.

As Tink searched, the sun sank and a thin sliver of moon rose in the sky. The night was so dark that even if Tink had flown over the hammer, she wouldn't have been able to see it.

Tink slowly started back to the Home Tree. What will I do without my hammer? she wondered. She

thought of the copper pot waiting
patiently for her in her workshop.

Tink knew that it wouldn't be easy
to get another tinker's hammer. A
tool-making fairy would need Never
iron to make a new hammer. And
a mining-talent fairy would have to
collect the iron. The mining-talent

fairies only mined when the moon
was full. Tink eyed the thin silver slice
in the sky. Judging from the moon's
size, that wouldn't be for many days.

But that wasn't the only reason she
was upset. Tink had a secret. She did
have a spare hammer. But it was at
Peter Pan's hideout. And she was terribly
scared about going back to get it.

Tink was too upset to go inside
the Home Tree and sleep. Instead,
she flew up to the highest branch and
looked up at the stars.

Tink thought about Peter Pan and
her heart ached. Remembering Peter
Pan was something she almost never
let herself do. Since he had brought

Wendy to Never Land, Tink and Peter had hardly spoken.

Tink decided she couldn't go to Peter's for the spare hammer. "I'll make do without it," she told herself. What was a hammer, after all, but just another tool?

3

The next morning, Tink awoke before the other fairies. She crept out of the Home Tree and flew down to the beach.

In one corner of the lagoon, there was a small cave that could only be entered at low tide. Tink flew in and landed on the damp ground. The floor of the cave was covered with sea-polished pebbles.

Tink carefully picked her way through the rocks. They were all smooth and shiny with seawater. At last Tink picked up a reddish pebble the size and shape of a sunflower seed.

"This might work," Tink said.

As the tide rose and the waves began to roll in, Tink flew out of the cave, gripping the pebble in her fist.

Back in her workshop, Tink used iron wire to bind the flat side of the rock to a twig. She held up her makeshift hammer.

"It's not so bad," she said.

Taking a deep breath, Tink began to tap the copper pot.

Clank! Clank! Clank! Tink winced as the horrible sound echoed through her workshop. With each blow, the copper pot seemed to shudder.

"I'm sorry, I'm sorry!" Tink said to

the pot. She tried to tap more gently.

Slowly, the bent copper straightened out. But the pot's smooth, shiny surface was now scarred by tiny dents.

Suddenly, the door of Tink's workshop burst open and Violet, the pot's owner, flew in.

"Tink! Thank goodness you're almost done with the – Oh!" Violet exclaimed. She stopped and stared at the pot in Tink's hands.

"Oh, Violet, hi. Yes, I'm, er... I'm done with the pot. That is, mostly," Tink said. She tugged nervously at her bangs. "It needs a couple of touch-ups, but I fixed the squashed part."

The door of Tink's workshop

opened again. Terence came in carrying a ladle that looked as if it had been tied in a knot.

"Hi, Tink! I brought you a ladle to fix!" he called out. "Oh, hello, Violet! Dropping off?" he asked when he saw the copper pot.

"No... er, picking up," Violet said.

"Oh," said Terence in surprise.

Tink brought a bucket of water over to her worktable. As Violet and Terence watched, she poured the water into the copper pot.

"See?" Tink said to Violet. "It's good as –"

Plink, plink, plink, plink! One by one, tiny streams of water burst

through the damaged copper.

"Oh!" Violet and Terence gasped.

Tink felt herself blush. She had never failed to fix a pot before, much less make it worse than it was when she got it.

4

After a long, awkward silence, Violet cleared her throat, and said, "I can probably share a dye pot with someone else. I'll come back and get this later."

Terence set the twisted ladle down on Tink's workbench.

"Tink, you look tired," he said gently.

"I'm not tired," said Tink.

"Maybe you need to take a break," Terence suggested. "On my way here, I smelled pumpkin muffins baking –"

"I'm not hungry," Tink interrupted, although she was starving. She hadn't had breakfast, or dinner the night before.

Suddenly, Tink was irritated with Terence. If he hadn't told her about the tag game, she never would have lost her hammer.

"I can't talk today, Terence," she snapped. "I have a lot of work and I'm already behind."

"Oh." Terence's shoulders sagged. He headed for the door. "Bye, Tink."

As soon as Terence was gone, Tink

went in search of a carpenter-talent
sparrow man and asked if she could
borrow his hammer. The sparrow man
agreed. He was in the middle of cutting
oak slats for some repairs in the Home
Tree and wouldn't need the hammer
until he was through.

When Tink returned to her
workshop, there was a sweet smell in
the air. She spied a pumpkin muffin
on a plate and a cup of buttermilk on
her workbench.

Terence, Tink thought. She felt
sorry that she'd snapped at him earlier.

As soon as she'd eaten, Tink
felt better.

She picked up the carpenter's

hammer and began to work on a stack of pie pans. The pans weren't cracked or dented, but Dulcie, the baking-talent fairy who'd brought them to her, complained that the pies she baked in them kept burning.

Tink worked slowly. The carpenter's hammer was almost twice as big as her tinker's hammer. She reshaped the pie pans, then added an extra layer of tin to the bottom of each one. When she was done, she looked over her work.

It's not the best job I've ever done, she thought. But it's not so bad, either.

Tink brought the pie pans to Dulcie, who was delighted to have them back.

"Don't miss tea this afternoon, Tink," she said with a wink as she brushed flour from her hands. "We're making strawberry pie. I'll save you an extra-big slice!"

On the way back to her workshop, Tink ran into Prilla, a young fairy with a freckled nose and a bouncy nature.

"Tink!" Prilla cried. "Did you hear?"

"Hear what?" asked Tink.

"About Queen Ree's tub," Prilla told

her. Ree was the fairies' nickname for their queen, Clarion. "It's sprung a leak."

Tink's eyes widened. The bathtub was one of Queen Ree's most prized possessions. It was made of Never pewter, and had morning glory leaves carved into its sides.

"The queen's attendants looked all over, but they couldn't spot the leak. I thought of you, Tink, when I heard," Prilla said. "Of course, Queen Ree will want you to fix it. You're the best."

Tink grinned back. It was the first time she'd smiled since she lost her hammer. "I hope so, Prilla. It would be quite an honour to work on the queen's tub," she replied.

Prilla turned a one-handed cartwheel and flew on. "See you later, Tink!" she called.

All afternoon, as she fixed the spout on a tea kettle that wouldn't whistle, Tink thought about the queen's tub.

By the time Tink had finished fixing the kettle, it was nearly teatime.

"They'll need this in the kitchen," Tink said to herself. She thought of the strawberry pie Dulcie had mentioned. Tink's stomach rumbled hungrily at the thought.

But when she got to the kitchen, a horrible smell greeted her. Tink quickly handed the teakettle to one of the cooking-talent fairies and held both hands to her nose. She made

her way through the kitchen until she found Dulcie. She was standing over several steaming pies that had just been pulled from the oven. She looked as if she might cry.

"Dulcie, what's going on?" Tink asked.

As soon as Dulcie saw Tink, her forehead wrinkled. "Oh, Tink," Dulcie said. "It's the pies. They're all coming out mincemeat."

Tink turned and looked at the steaming pies.

"We tried everything," Dulcie went on. "When the strawberry came out all wrong, we tried plum. When that didn't work, we tried cherry. We even tried pumpkin. But every time we pulled the pies out of the oven, they'd turned into mincemeat."

"Is there something wrong with the oven?" Tink asked Dulcie.

Dulcie swallowed hard.

"No, Tink," she said slowly. "It's the pans you fixed. Only the pies baked in those pans are the ones that get spoiled."

5

Before Tink could say
anything, a shrill whistle split the air.

The tea water had boiled. A
cooking-talent sparrow man hurried
over to lift the kettle off the fire.
Then he poured the water into the
teacups until there wasn't a drop left.

But the teakettle continued to
shriek. The sparrow man lifted the
kettle's lid to let out any steam that

might have been caught inside, but the kettle still whistled on.

All the fairies in the kitchen, including Tink, covered their ears. Several fairies who were in the tearoom poked their heads into the kitchen doorway.

"What's all that noise?" a garden-talent fairy asked one of the baking-talent fairies.

"It's the teakettle, the one that just wouldn't whistle," the baking-talent fairy replied. "Tink fixed it, and now it won't shut up!"

Twee-twee-tweeeeeeeeee! the teakettle shrieked cheerfully.

"And the pie pans Tink fixed

aren't any good, either," another baking-talent fairy noted over the noise. "Every pie baked in them turns into mincemeat!"

Everyone turned and looked at Tink.

Tink stared back at them, blushing so deeply her glow turned orange. Then, without thinking, she turned and fled.

Tink was sitting in the shade of a wild rosebush, deep in thought. She didn't notice Vidia, a fast-flying-talent fairy, until she landed right in front of her.

"Tinker Bell, darling," Vidia greeted her.

"Hello, Vidia," Tink replied as kindly as she could. Vidia was selfish and mean-spirited, and at the moment she was smiling in a way Tink didn't like at all.

"I'm so sorry to hear about your trouble," Vidia said.

Tink shrugged. "I'll go fix the teakettle now."

"Oh, don't worry about that. Angus got the teakettle to stop," Vidia said. Angus was a pots-and-pans sparrow man. "What I meant was, I'm sorry to hear about your *talent*."

Tink blinked. "What do you mean?"

"Oh, don't you know?" Vidia

asked. "Everyone's talking about how you've lost your talent."

"What?" Tink leaped to her feet.

"It's a shame, really," Vidia went on. "You were always such a good little tinker."

"I haven't lost my talent," Tink growled.

"If you say so. But you have to admit, your work hasn't exactly been... inspired lately," Vidia pointed out. "But I wouldn't worry too much. I'm sure they won't make you leave Pixie Hollow forever."

Tink looked at her in dismay.

Vidia gave Tink a pitying smile. "But no one really knows, do they? After all,

no fairy has ever lost her talent before. But I guess we'll soon find out. The queen would like to see you."

Tink's stomach did a little flip. Her heart raced. Was it really possible that she could be banished from Pixie Hollow for losing her talent?

But I haven't lost my *talent!* Tink thought indignantly. I've just lost my *hammer.*

Tink took a deep breath, lifted her chin and flew off to meet the queen.

6

As she made her way to the queen's gazebo, Tink passed a group of harvest-talent fairies. They laughed and chatted as they worked, but as soon as they saw Tink, they all stopped talking.

Tink scowled as she flew past another group of fairies who silently gawked at her. She had always hated gossip and now she hated it even more.

The queen's gazebo sat high on a rock overlooking Pixie Hollow. Tink landed lightly on a bed of soft moss outside the entrance. All around her she heard the jingle of seashell wind chimes, which hung around the gazebo.

Queen Ree stood at one of the open windows, looking out. When she heard Tink, she turned.

"Tinker Bell, come in," said the queen.

Tink stepped inside. She waited.

"Tink, how are you feeling?" Queen Ree asked.

"I'm fine," Tink replied.

"Tink, you know there are

rumours…" Queen Ree hesitated.

"They say I've lost my talent," Tink said quickly. "It's nasty gossip and untrue. It's just that –" Tink stopped. She tugged at her hair.

She was afraid that if she told Queen Ree about her missing hammer, the queen would think she was irresponsible.

The queen waited for Tink to go on. Finally, she said, "Tink, is there anything you want to tell me?"

Tink suddenly felt the urge to tell her everything – about the pebble hammer and the carpenter's hammer and even about Peter Pan. But Tink had never told another fairy about

Peter, and she was afraid to now.

Besides, Tink told herself, the queen has more important things to worry about than a missing hammer.

Tink shook her head. "No," she said. "I'm sorry my pots and pans haven't been very good lately. I'll try to do better."

"Very well," Queen Ree said. As Tink turned to leave, she added, "Be good to yourself, Tink."

Tink felt better after her meeting with the queen. All I have to do now is find a new hammer and everything will be back to normal, Tink thought with a burst of confidence.

"Tink!" someone called.

She looked down and saw Rani and Prilla standing knee-deep in a puddle. Tink flew down and landed at the edge.

"What are you doing?" she asked.

"Rani's showing me how she makes fountains in the water," Prilla explained. "I thought it might be fun to try in Clumsy children's lemonade." Prilla's talent was travelling over to the mainland and visiting the children there. She was the only fairy in all of Never Land who had this talent, and it was an important one. She helped keep up children's belief in fairies.

"I've been trying all afternoon, but this is all I can do," Prilla told her. She took a pinch of fairy dust and sprinkled it onto the water. After a moment, a few small bubbles rose to the surface and popped.

Prilla sighed. "Now watch Rani."

Rani sprinkled a pinch of fairy dust on the water. Instantly, a ten-centimetre fountain of water shot up from the puddle.

Tink and Prilla clapped their hands and cheered.

Just then, Tink heard a snuffling sound. She saw that Rani was crying.

"I'm so sorry, Tink," Rani said. She pulled a damp leafkerchief from one of her many pockets and blew her nose into it. "About your talent, I mean."

Tink's smile faded. She tugged at her hair. "There's nothing wrong with my talent," she said irritably.

"Don't worry, Tink," Prilla said. "I know how you feel. When I thought I didn't have a talent, it was awful. Maybe you just need to try lots of different things."

"I already have a talent, Prilla," Tink said carefully.

"But maybe you need another talent, to have a back-up when the one you have isn't working," Prilla went on.

Tink tugged her hair so hard that a few blonde hairs came out in her fingers.

"Dinner?" Rani said loudly.

Prilla looked at her strangely. "What?"

Rani had dried her eyes and now she was looking hard at Prilla. She could see that the topic of talents was upsetting Tink, and she wanted Prilla to be quiet. "It's time, isn't it?"

"Yes," said Tink. She took off in the direction of the Home Tree without another word. Rani and Prilla had no choice but to follow.

7

When she reached the tearoom, Tink made her way over to a table under a large chandelier. It was where the pots-and-pans fairies sat. As she took her seat, the other fairies at the table barely looked up.

"It's a crack in the bottom, I'll bet," a fairy named Zuzu was saying. "I mended a pewter bowl once that that'd had boiling water poured into it when it was cold. A crack had formed right down the centre."

Tink leaned forward. "What's everyone talking about?" she asked.

The other fairies turned, as if noticing her for the first time.

"About Queen Ree's bathtub," Zuzu explained. "She's asked us to go and fix it tomorrow. We're trying to guess what's wrong with it."

"Oh, yes!" said Tink. "I've been thinking about that too. It might be a pinprick hole. Those are the sneakiest sorts of leaks – the water just sort of drizzles out one drop at a time." Tink laughed.

But no one joined her. She glanced

around the table. The other fairies were awkwardly looking down at their soup bowls.

"Tink," another fairy named Copper said gently, "we've all agreed that Angus and Zuzu should be the ones to repair the tub, since they are the most talented pots-and-pans fairies... lately, that is."

"Oh!" said Tink. "Of course." She swallowed hard.

Now all the pots-and-pans fairies were looking at Tink with a mixture of love and concern. And, Tink was sad to see, pity.

At last, the fairies changed the topic and began to talk about the leaky pots and broken teakettles they'd fixed that day. As they chattered and laughed, Tink silently ate her soup.

As soon as she was finished eating, Tink put down her spoon and slipped away from the table.

Outside, Tink returned to the topmost branches of the Home Tree. She didn't want to go back to her workshop where there were pots and pans still waiting to be fixed. She didn't want to go to her room, either. At least here she had the stars to keep her company.

"Maybe it's true that I've lost my talent," Tink said to the stars. "If I don't have a hammer, then I can't fix things. And if I can't fix things, it's just like having no talent at all."

From where she was sitting, Tink could see the hawthorn tree where Mother Dove lived. Mother Dove was the only creature in Pixie Hollow who knew all about Tink and Peter Pan.

Mother Dove had once told Tinker Bell that she was brave enough for anything.

But Tink didn't feel very brave right now, certainly not brave enough to go to Peter's hideout and get her spare hammer.

"Tink," said a voice.

Tink turned. Terence was standing behind her on the branch. She'd been so wrapped up in her thoughts, she hadn't even heard him fly up.

"I haven't fixed the ladle yet," Tink told him miserably.

"I didn't come because of the ladle," Terence replied. "I saw you leave the tearoom."

Terence sat down next to her on the branch. "Tink, are you all right? Everyone is saying that..."

"That I've lost my talent," Tink finished for him. She sighed. "Maybe they're right, Terence. I can't seem to fix anything anymore."

Terence was startled. He had never seen her look as defeated as she did now.

"I don't believe that," he told her. "You're the best pots-and-pans fairy in Pixie Hollow. Talent doesn't just go away like that."

Tink didn't say anything. But she felt grateful to him for not believing the rumours – for still believing in her.

"Tink," Terence asked gently, "what's really going on?"

Tink hesitated. "I lost my hammer," she blurted out. She felt relieved. It was as if she'd let out a huge breath that she'd been holding in.

Tink told Terence about the hammer she'd made from a pebble and the one she'd borrowed from the carpenter fairy. Then she took a deep breath and said, "I have a spare. But it's... I... I left it at Peter Pan's hideout."

Terence didn't know much about Peter Pan, only that Tink had been friends with him and then – suddenly – she wasn't. But he saw that Tink was upset, and he didn't ask her anything more.

"I could go with you," Terence said.

Tink's mind raced. "You would do that?" she asked. Perhaps if someone else came along, it wouldn't be so hard to see Peter...

"Tink," said Terence, "I'm your friend. You don't even need to ask."

He gave Tink a sparkling smile. This time, she saw it and smiled back.

8

Early the next morning,
Tink rapped on the door to Terence's
room. She wanted to leave for
Peter's hideout before she lost her
nerve altogether.

Terence threw open the door after
the first knock. He grinned at Tink.
"Ready to go get your talent back,
Tinker Bell?"

Tink smiled. She was glad Terence

was going with her, and not just because it would be easier with someone else along.

They left Pixie Hollow just as the sun's rays shone over Torth Mountain.

"See that peak?" Tink told Terence. She pointed out a chair-shaped spot at the top of a hill. "That's called the Throne. When the Lost Boys have their skirmishes, the winner is named king of the hill.

"And that stream," she went on, pointing to a silver ribbon of water winding through the forest below, "leads to an underground cavern that's filled with gold and silver. Captain Hook and his men have hidden

away a whole pirate ship's worth of treasure there."

"You must know Never Land better than any fairy in Pixie Hollow," Terence said admiringly.

Tink looked down at the island below her and felt a little twinge of pride. What Terence said was true. With Peter Pan and the Lost Boys, Tink had explored nearly every inch of Never Land.

When Tink reached the densest, darkest part of the forest, she began to glide down in a spiral. Terence followed her.

They plunged through a canopy of fig trees and landed on a white-speckled mushroom.

"It's Peter's hideout," Tink explained. "They use a mushroom cap to disguise the chimney so they can fool Captain Hook."

Peeking inside, Terence saw that the entire tree was hollow, right to its roots. He followed Tink as she flew down the trunk. They came out in an underground room.

Terence looked around. The floor and walls were made of packed earth. Tree roots hung down from the ceiling, and from these, string hammocks dangled limply. Here and there on the ground lay slingshots, socks and dirty coconut-shell bowls.

The remains of a fire smoldered in a corner.

But the hideout was empty.

Just then, they heard whistling coming from somewhere near the back of the den.

Tink and Terence flew toward the sound.

When they rounded a corner, Terence saw a boy with a mop of red hair sitting on a stool. In one hand he held a jackknife. He whistled as he worked the knife over a piece of wood, carving a large hook. A fishing pole leaned against the wall behind him.

Tink saw her old friend, Peter Pan. Taking a deep breath, Tink said,

"Hello, Peter."

But Peter didn't seem to hear her. He continued to whistle and chip away at the wood.

Tink flew a little bit closer. "Peter!" she exclaimed.

Then Terence took her hand. They flew up to Peter until they were just a few inches from his face. "Peter!" they both cried.

Peter lifted his head. When he saw them, a bright smile lit his face.

"What's this?" Peter said. "Two butterflies have come to visit me!"

Tink's smile faded. Butterflies?

Peter squinted at them. "You're awful pretty. I just love butterflies," he said. "You'd make a fine addition to my collection. Let's see now, where are my pins?"

He began to search his pockets. As he did, small items fell onto the ground beneath his seat: a parrot feather, a snail shell, a bit of string.

"Here it is!" he cried. He held up a straight pin with a coloured bulb on the end. It was big enough to skewer a butterfly – or a fairy – right through the middle.

"Now hold still," Peter said. Gripping the pin in one hand, he reached up to grab Tink and Terence with the other.

"Fly!" Terence screamed to Tink.

Just before Peter's stubby fingers

closed around them, the fairies turned
and fled toward the exit.

9

As Tinker Bell and Terence reached the roots of the jackfruit tree, they heard a whoop of laughter behind them.

Tink stopped and glanced back over her shoulder. Peter was clutching his stomach and shaking with laughter.

"Oh, Tink!" he gasped. "You should have seen the looks on your faces. Butterflies! Oh, I am funny. Oh, oh."

At last Peter stopped laughing. He bounded up to Tink and Terence, his eyes shining.

"Tink!" he cried. "It's awful great to see you. Where've you been hiding?"

"Hello, Peter," Tink replied. "Meet my friend Terence."

"A boy pixie! Fantastic!" Peter cried, turning to stare at Terence. "You'll never guess what I've got, Tink," he continued. "Come see!"

Peter pulled a wooden cigar box out of a hole in the wall.

"I keep my most important things in a treasure chest," Peter explained to Terence, gesturing to the box.

Peter lifted the lid of the cigar box.

Reaching inside, he took out a small object. He held it out toward Tink and Terence in the palm of his hand. It was yellowish white and shaped like a triangle, with razor-sharp edges that narrowed to a point.

Tink clasped her hands together. "Oh!" she gasped. "You got it!"

"What is it?" Terence asked.

"A shark's tooth," Peter replied, just a bit smugly.

"The first time I met Peter, he was trying to steal a shark's tooth," Tink explained to Terence.

"That's right!" exclaimed Peter. "I'd made a bet with the Lost Boys that I could steal a tooth from a live shark."

"So, you went back and got the shark tooth this time?" Tink asked Peter, pointing to the tooth in his hand.

Peter shrugged. "Naw. A mermaid gave this to me. But now I'm going to go out and get the whole shark!" He pointed to the fishing pole and the wooden hook he'd been carving.

Tink and Peter both burst out laughing.

Terence smiled, watching them. He felt glad that Tink looked so happy. But it also made him sad. What if she decided to stay here in the forest with Peter?

Tink was happy. She had discovered that it wasn't so hard to see Peter, after all! She'd only needed a friend to help her find that out. She smiled at Terence.

Just then, Tink caught sight of something in the cigar box. Her

eyes widened. "My hammer!"
she exclaimed.

"I saved it for you, Tink," Peter said proudly. "I knew you'd be back for it."

Tink reached into the box and picked up the hammer. It fit perfectly in her hand.

Then, to Terence's joy and relief, Tink turned to Peter and said, "It's been so good to see you, Peter. But we have to go back to Pixie Hollow."

Peter looked at her in surprise. "What? Now? But what about hide-and-seek?"

Tink shook her head sadly at her old friend. She didn't want to play games with Peter anymore. She wanted to get back to her workshop where her pots and pans were waiting. That was where she belonged.

Tink flew so close to Peter's face that he had to cross his eyes to see her. She kissed the bridge of his freckled nose. "I'll come back soon to visit," she promised. And she meant it.

Then, taking Terence's hand, she flew back out of the jackfruit tree and into the forest.

10

As Tink headed back to
Pixie Hollow with Terence, one last
thing was bothering her.

She didn't want all of Pixie Hollow
to know about the spare hammer and
her trip to see Peter. Before she could
say anything to Terence, he turned to
her. "I don't think anyone else needs
to know about this trip, do you?" he
asked. "You've got your hammer back,

and that's what matters."

Tink grinned and nodded. What a good friend Terence was.

When they got to the Home Tree, Tink went straight to Queen Ree's quarters.

One of the queen's attendants opened the door. "Tink, welcome," she said.

"I've come to fix the queen's bathtub," Tink told her.

Terence, who was standing behind Tink, grinned. This was the perfect way to prove that her talent was back.

Queen Ree stepped forward. "Come in, Tinker Bell," she said.

"I've come to fix your bathtub," Tink repeated to the queen.

Ree looked at Tink. In Tink's blue eyes, she saw a fierce certainty that hadn't been there the day before.

The Queen nodded. "Take Tink to the bathtub," she told her attendant.

Just before Tink left, Terence grabbed her hand. "Good luck," he said.

Tink held up her hammer and gave his hand a squeeze. "I don't need it!" she replied.